DR. THIRTEENTH
originated by Roger Hargreaves

Written and illustrated by Adam Hargreaves

Yaz was very excited.

It was the day before her birthday and she wondered what the Doctor and Ryan and Graham had planned.

She had no idea.

Funnily enough, the Doctor and Ryan and Graham had no idea, either.

What could they do for Yaz's birthday?

"How about a cake?" suggested Ryan.

"And candles and balloons?" added Graham.

"Hmm. That's all a bit predictable, isn't it?" said the Doctor.

"Not if it's a surprise birthday party," said Graham.

"And not if it's a very cool cake and very cool candles and very cool balloons," added Ryan.

"But where will we get those?" asked the Doctor.

"Well," said Graham, "we thought that would be your job, Doc."

"After all," added Ryan, "we've done the hard part, coming up with an idea!"

The Doctor groaned.

But she wanted to make Yaz's birthday special, so off she set in the TARDIS.

She flew across space to the planet of Sontar, where she had heard there was a bakery.

Which was a bit of a surprise, as the Sontarans were a terrible, warlike people who liked nothing better than fighting.

She bought a cake. A Sontaran Frosted Boom Cake.

"What is a Boom Cake?" asked the Doctor.

"A cake with a surprise in it," explained the baker.

"A surprise cake for a surprise party," said the Doctor. "That is perfect!"

The Sontaran baker smiled.

The Doctor set off again in the TARDIS in search of candles and balloons.

She went back in time to London.

Back in time to the 1940s and the Blitz. Where she found some balloons.

Some enormous balloons!

The balloons were so big that they slowed the TARDIS down as it traveled above London.

The TARDIS flew even further back in time to Paris.

An old-fashioned Paris, lit by candles. Where the Doctor found just what she was looking for.

The Doctor then flew forward through time, back to Graham and Ryan.

They could not believe their eyes as the TARDIS came in to land, trailing the huge balloons.

And they were even more taken aback when they saw the cake and the candles.

The cake had begun to bubble and froth.

"What is that?" exclaimed Ryan.

"It's a Sontaran Frosted Boom Cake," said the Doctor, proudly.

"And do you think a Boom Cake is a good idea?" asked Graham.

But it was too late to argue.

Yaz had arrived.

"Happy surprise birthday!" cried the Doctor and Ryan and Graham in unison.

And with her sonic screwdriver, the Doctor lit the candles she had placed on the cake.

It exploded with an enormous . . .

Covering the TARDIS team in pink chocolate!

"Maybe that's a happy BOOMday?" laughed the Doctor.

"I have to say, this tastes pretty good," chuckled Yaz.